Making and Using a Rain Gauge

Heather Hammonds

Photographs by Lindsay Edwards

Contents

Measuring the Rain

At some times of the year, it rains a lot. At other times, it may rain less.

A rain gauge is a tool that can be used to measure **rainfall**.

Scientists find out information about rainfall from rain gauges.
They use the information to make rainfall graphs.
They study the graphs to see how much rain falls over days, months and years.

You can make your own rain gauge and use it, too!

Scientists check the water level in a rain gauge.

Goals

- To make and use a rain gauge to measure how much rain falls
- To draw some rainfall graphs

Materials

You will need:

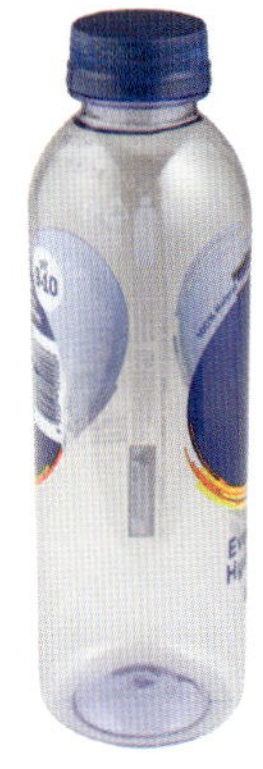

- a plastic bottle with a flat bottom

- another plastic bottle that is wider than the first
- a permanent marker

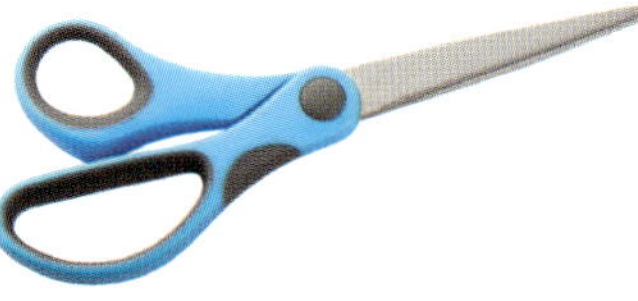

- a pair of scissors

- **waterproof** tape

- a 30 cm ruler

- a **bamboo** stake

- a hammer

- a notebook and pencil

- graph paper

- seven coloured markers.

Steps

Making the Rain Gauge

1. Take the tops off the bottles.
2. Rinse the bottles with water, so they are clean.
3. Peel the labels off the bottles.

4. Make a mark on the smaller bottle, about one quarter of the way from the top.

5. Ask an adult to cut around the bottle with scissors, where you made the mark.

The bottle will now be in two pieces.
You will have a top part and a bottom part.

6. Cut two pieces of waterproof tape.
Make them long enough to go around the cut edges of the top and bottom parts of the small bottle.

7. Ask an adult to fold the tape over the cut edges of the two parts of the bottle, for safety.

8. Turn the top part of the bottle upside-down and put it inside the bottom part, to make a **funnel**.
9. Check that the funnel fits neatly inside the bottle.

10. Now take the funnel out of the bottle again.

Hold the ruler against the outside of the bottle.

Use the permanent marker to draw
10 lines on the bottle, from bottom to top.
Make the lines 1 cm apart.

11. Then draw a small line in between each bigger line.

Number the bigger lines from 10 mm to 100 mm.

12. Put the funnel back inside the bottle.
Stick it to the bottle with one small piece of tape.
Now the funnel will not blow off in the wind.

The rain gauge is complete.

Rainfall is measured in millimetres (mm).
There are 10 millimetres in each centimetre (cm).

Making a Holder for Your Rain Gauge

1. Ask an adult to cut the bigger bottle so it is in two halves.

2. Put the top half in the recycling bin. The bottom half will be the holder for the rain gauge.

3. Check that the top of the rain gauge sticks out of the top of the holder. Then it can collect rain.

4. Take the rain gauge out of the holder. Then, ask an adult to cut two holes in the bottom of the holder. When it rains, water that falls in the holder will empty out through the holes.

5. Cut a piece of waterproof tape, long enough to go around the top of the holder.

6. Ask an adult to fold the tape over the sharp edge of the holder.

7. Cut two more pieces of tape, long enough to go all the way around the holder.
8. Stick the holder to the top of the bamboo stake with the tape.
9. Put the rain gauge inside its holder.

Using Your Rain Gauge

1. Take the rain gauge outside.
   Keep it away from fences, trees or buildings, so it can collect lots of rain.

2. Ask an adult to use the hammer to push the stake into the ground, so the rain gauge stays **upright**.

Now, you can use the rain gauge to measure rainfall.

3. Check the rain gauge at the same time every morning.
4. Write the day of the week and the date in the notebook. 
5. Write down how much rain was collected.

6. Open the funnel of your rain gauge and tip the water out.

7. Close the funnel again.

Now the rain gauge is ready to collect more rain.

Making a Rainfall Graph

1. Measure the rainfall every morning for two weeks.
2. At the top of a piece of graph paper, write the dates that you measured the rainfall on.

3. Write the names of 14 days along the bottom of the graph.

4. Write the numbers 10 to 100 up the side of the graph paper.

5. Write mm (for millimetres) above the numbers and Days below the days of the week.

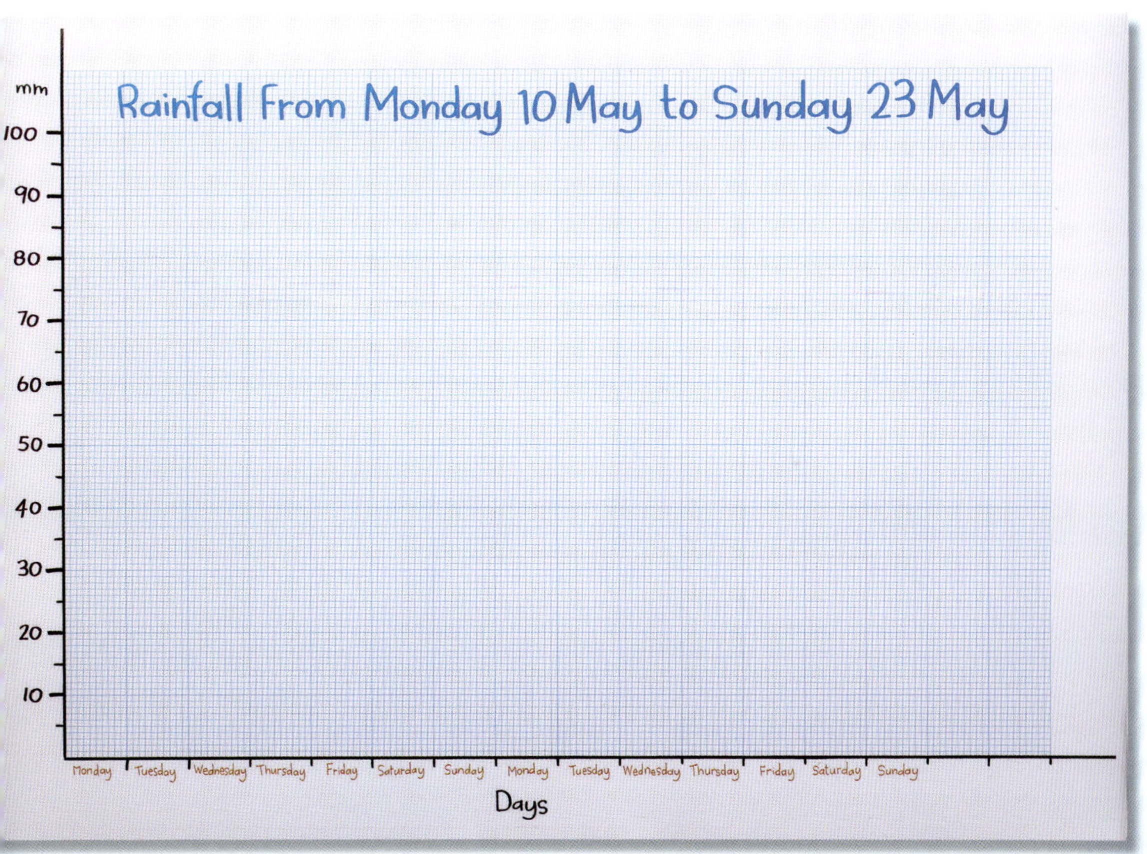

6. Choose a coloured marker for each day of the week.

7. Look at the information recorded in the notebook. Then, colour in squares on the graph to show how much rain fell each day.

8. Study the graph when you have finished it.
See which days were wettest.

Glossary

bamboo (*noun*)	a kind of tall grass that can be dried out
funnel (*noun*)	a tool with a large open top and a thin pipe underneath, used for pouring water into a bottle
rainfall (*noun*)	the amount of rain that has fallen at one place
upright (*adjective*)	standing up straight
waterproof (*adjective*)	allowing no water to enter or pass through